This book
belongs to:

_____

This book
belongs to

I Can Jump

A LEARN TO READ BOOK

By Darlene Freeman
Illustrated by Heidi Petach

 **CHECKERBOARD PRESS**
NEW YORK

Copyright © 1989 Checkerboard Press, a division of Macmillan, Inc. All rights reserved.
ISBN 002-898253-3 Printed in U.S.A. Library of Congress Catalog Card Number: 89-7242

CHECKERBOARD PRESS and colophon, BIG & EASY and elephant logo, are trademarks of Macmillan, Inc.

0 9 8 7 6 5 4 3 2 1

jump

I can jump.

frog

A frog can jump.

dog

A dog can jump.

snail

Can a snail jump?

kangaroo

Can a kangaroo jump?

monkey

Can a monkey jump?

turtle

Can a turtle jump?

Who can jump?